CLEVER CUB

Learns about Love

Bob Hartman
Illustrated by Steve Brown

DAVID C COOK

transforming lives together

CLEVER CUB LEARNS ABOUT LOVE
Published by David C Cook
4050 Lee Vance Drive
Colorado Springs, CO 80918 U.S.A.

Integrity Music Limited, a Division of David C Cook
Brighton, East Sussex BN1 2RE, England

The graphic circle C logo is a registered trademark of David C Cook.

Library of Congress Control Number 2021936134
ISBN 978-0-8307-8253-6

© 2021 Bob Hartman
Illustrations by Steve Brown. Copyright © 2021 David C Cook

The Team: Laura Derico, Stephanie Bennett, Judy Gillispie, James Hershberger
Cover Design: James Hershberger
Cover Art: Steve Brown

Printed in China
First Edition 2021

1 2 3 4 5 6 7 8 9 10

062921

Mama Bear and Clever Cub sat by the river
at the end of a long, happy day.
"I **LOVE YOU**, Mama Bear," said Clever Cub.

"I love you too," Mama Bear replied.
She gave her little cub a **BIG** bear hug.

"There are many ways to say 'I love you,' you know."

3

"I know," said Clever Cub. He picked up a pinecone and handed it to his mama. "You can give someone a PRESENT!"

4

"Thank you," Mama Bear said with a smile.
"That is a very **SNAZZY** pinecone!
But there are other ways too.
This river reminds me of a story about one of them."

5

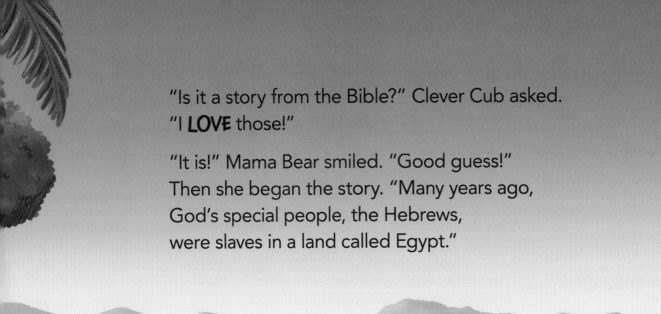

"Is it a story from the Bible?" Clever Cub asked.
"I **LOVE** those!"

"It is!" Mama Bear smiled. "Good guess!"
Then she began the story. "Many years ago,
God's special people, the Hebrews,
were slaves in a land called Egypt."

"What were slaves?" asked Clever Cub.

"Slaves were people who had to work for nothing.
They were not free to do what they wanted to do.
They had to do just what their masters told them to do.
Their lives were very, **VERY** hard."

"The thing is, God blessed His people
with more and more children.
And that worried Pharaoh, the ruler of Egypt.
'There are too **MANY** Hebrews!' he said.
'And soon they will be too **MIGHTY**!
If we are not careful, they will take over our land.'
So he made a terrible, horrible rule."

Clever Cub listened hard. He pulled his ear.
He did that sometimes when he was worried.
Mama Bear whispered, "Pharaoh's rule said this:
Every baby Hebrew boy must be thrown into the Nile River."

"**OH NO**!" Clever Cub gasped. "That is **TERRIBLE**!
And **HORRIBLE** too!" He pulled both ears.

"It was!" Mama Bear nodded. "But one Hebrew mama had a plan ..."

"A **CLEVER** plan?" asked Clever Cub.

"Very clever!" Mama Bear replied. "She made a basket out of the tall, strong reeds that grew by the river. She made it big enough to hold her baby boy. Then she covered the basket with tar, so the water wouldn't get inside. And what do you think she did next?"

"Did she put her baby in the **BASKET**?" Clever Cub asked.

"She did! You *are* a clever cub! And she was a clever mama.
She put the baby boy she loved so much in the basket to save him.
Then she set the basket floating in the water, among the river reeds."

"Hmmm." Clever Cub was thinking hard.
"That clever mama saved her boy from being hurt
by Pharaoh's terrible, horrible rule.
Is that how she said 'I love you'?" asked Clever Cub.

"Yes, it is." Mama Bear smiled. "But there's more.

Someone needed to keep an eye on that basket.
The river was full of dangers—
snake **BITES** and hippo **STOMPS** and crocodile **CHOMPS**.
But that baby boy had a big sister. And she was **BRAVE**.
She went down by the dangerous river,
and she watched over her brother. She made sure
that nothing bad happened to him."

"Ohhh," Clever Cub said. "I bet that was **SCARY**, down there with the snakes and the hippos and the crocodiles. And with all the gnats and mosquitoes—it was probably **ITCHY**!" Clever Cub squirmed and wriggled. He was feeling itchy now too!

14

"I'm sure it was," Mama Bear nodded.
"But even though it wasn't easy,
she did what she could to protect her baby brother."

"And that's love too?" asked Clever Cub.

"It is," replied his mama. "But there's even **MORE**!"

"One day, Pharaoh's own daughter went down to the Nile.
Back then, even princesses used the river water for their baths,
just like we bears do!" Clever Cub looked surprised.

"While the princess was there,
she spotted the basket.
She sent her servants to bring it to her."

"**OH NO!**" Clever Cub said.

"I'm sure that's what the baby's sister
thought too," said Mama Bear.

"When Pharaoh's daughter looked inside the basket, she saw the baby. She knew he was a Hebrew child."

Clever Cub hid his eyes. "Did she throw him into the river like her father told the Egyptians to do?!"

"**NO**, she didn't!" Mama Bear said. "The baby cried,
and the princess felt sorry for him. She wanted to take care of him.
Then the baby's sister was brave again. She walked right up
to the princess and said, 'Shall I get a Hebrew woman
to feed the baby for you?' The princess nodded and said, '**GO**!'
The girl went right away and …"

"Told her mama!" Clever Cub shouted.

"**YES**, she did!" Mama Bear said. "And the Hebrew mama cared for her baby boy until he was old enough to live in Pharaoh's palace with the princess. But he was still a Hebrew boy. He was still in **DANGER**.

The princess decided to adopt the baby as her very own son to keep him **SAFE**. And that's when Pharaoh's daughter gave the boy his name: **MOSES**, which means 'I pulled him out of the water.'"

"And is that love too?" asked Clever Cub.

"Definitely!" Mama Bear nodded. "Her father saw the Hebrews as slaves and enemies. But the princess saw a precious person, just like her. And THAT is love."

"I love that story!" Clever Cub grinned. "And I'm going to see if I can pull something out of the river too!"

"Then I'd better come with you," Mama Bear replied.

"To watch over me and make sure nothing bad happens to me?" asked Clever Cub. "Because you love me?"

Mama Bear nodded. "Yes, definitely. Because **I LOVE YOU**."

23

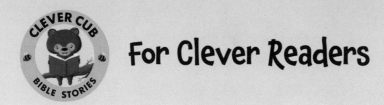

For Clever Readers

Clever Cub is a curious little bear who **LOVES** to cuddle up with the Bible and learn about God! In this story, Clever Cub hears from the Bible about a baby boy who was loved very much. You can read this same exciting story in Exodus 1 and 2:1–10. This story has some scary things in it, but we can always be sure that no matter what happens, God loves us and wants us to be safe.

When have you ever felt brave?
It's brave to show love for others even when it's hard to do.
How can you show love for someone today?